R E S C U E   Book 1

A Great Break

Reading Practice

ay	a–e	ai
day	fake	rain
pay	waves	pain
clay	amaze	chain
gray	save	fail
stay	hate	aim
tray	brave	stain
delay	chase	complain
		explain

a	ea	ey
crazy	great	they
lazy	steak	prey
baby	break	whey

Contents

"Gazing at the waves has helped me stay sane!" grinned Mom as they packed the van. "It's a shame it has to end!"

Contents

Vocabulary:

fantastic – great or amazing

gaze – to look at something with great interest

exclaim – to say with great excitement

mock – to tease

Chapter 1
Waves

Mom had taken Erin and baby Jack away. Mom had a job in a lab and it had been great to have a break. Ten hot days in the sun had been fantastic.

"Gazing at the waves has helped me stay sane!" grinned Mom as they packed the van. "It's a shame it has to end!"

"I hate to say it," Mom said to Erin when they got back, "but I must spend the rest of the day at the lab." Ten days was a long time to be away from her job.

Mom was involved in a big project. The lab had invented a shrink ray that was able to shrink bugs and pests. The shrink ray had once been robbed from the lab, so Mom kept it hidden at home.

Erin was babysitting Jack. She sat in the shade, with cold milkshakes, waiting for her best mate, Danny, to visit. Danny waved as he skated along.

Chapter 2
The Game

"Cold milkshake!" exclaimed Danny. "Great for such a hot day!"

"It's getting late," said Erin. "Jack will be awake soon. Let's play the space game."

It was a great game and they often played it when Danny came to visit.
"Race you to it!" yelled Danny as he jumped up.
"So brave of you to risk failing again," mocked Erin.

A sudden hiccup stopped them. Jack was waking up. Erin lifted him up and hugged him. "Mom left us a cake," she told him. "I'll get it."

Chapter 3
Jack Escapes!

Danny had to go. He gave baby Jack a quick kiss as he left. "You saved Erin from the pain of me winning again," he grinned.

Erin left Jack next to his bed, playing with his train set. The cake was on a plate on the kitchen table.

10

When she got back, Jack was not playing with his train! "Jack?" The tray and the cake dropped from her hands as she ran.

Jack had left a trail of milk splashes on his way to Mom's desk. Erin felt faint. The shrink ray was kept in a box by Mom's desk!

Chapter 4
The Shrink Ray

Erin raced to Mom's desk. The shrink ray lay on the mat, not safely in its box. When Erin picked it up, it felt hot in her hand.

Erin grabbed at the things on the desk.
No Jack. She lay flat on the mat.
Still no Jack. She was so afraid that
she began to shake.

A scrap of red cloth was next to Mom's desk. "It's Jack's sock, but it's as big as a doll's sock!" said Erin. "Jack must be as big as a snail!"

"Jack is still just a baby," said Erin. "He won't be safe. I must save him. I have to shrink as well." She gazed at the shrink ray. "Mom is going to go crazy..."

R E S C U E   Book 2
The Search Begins

Reading Practice

ee	ei	ie
need	seize	shriek
green	ceiling	believe
sweep	receive	shield
knee		grief
wheel		
squeeze		

ea	e-e	e	y
reach	Pete	me	quickly
sneak	these	he	safety
weaving	delete	she	teddy
steam		evil	sticky
beach		relax	empty
daydream			

Contents

Vocabulary:

grapple – a metal hook which connects one thing to another

shriek – to cry out loudly and sharply

seize – to take hold of something suddenly

weave – to move from side to side

lapping – to wash against something with a splashing sound

scan – to look at something quickly

replace – to put another in its place

squeeze – to fit into a small or crowded space

Chapter 1
A Plan

Erin needed to think quickly. If Jack was as big as a doll, then he was not safe. "I must collect all the things I'll need, and then shrink myself!"

Erin put Mom's keys next to the desk in case she needed to leave. Mom had a thick green liquid to reverse the effects of the shrink ray. Erin added that.

Erin reached into a pot on Mom's desk and picked up a rusty safety pin. She tied it to a lace from an old sneaker so that it made a strong grapple.

Jack had not eaten yet. Erin got candy from her bag, cut up an apple and filled a bottle lid with milk. "These will be a meal we can easily reach," she told herself.

Chapter 2
A Shrinking Feeling

When Erin picked up the shrink ray, it felt hot in her hand. She pressed the switch and a jet of evil-smelling steam shot from the end of it.

Suddenly, Erin was shrinking! It was such a funny feeling. "I am as big as Jack's bear!" she giggled, as she licked a sticky bit of candy. "This candy is as big as a beach ball!"

A pan of meat and beans was on the stove. Maybe Jack was hungry and went to the kitchen? Erin ran to see.

Chapter 3
The Beast in the Kitchen!

The kitchen seemed to be empty. Then a thud came from next to the sink. Maybe it was Jack? "Jack!" shrieked Erin as she ran to see. Sadly, it was not Jack. It was Erin's greedy cat, Ziggy.

Erin did not want the hungry cat to see her. She backed away quickly. "I need to get to the top of the sink," she said softly. She tossed the grapple up until it got stuck in a handle.

It was a long way to the top and Erin felt weak at the knees. "Relax and keep breathing," she told herself. "I'll pretend this is a tree on the beach." In her daydream, waves lapped gently on the sand.

The lapping waves were really in the sink! Pots and pans bobbed in streams of bubbles. Erin seized the rim of a tea cup and jumped in.

She paddled across the sink, weaving past the greasy pots. The tea cup rocked and Erin began to feel seasick. It was a relief to reach solid land next to the sink.

She scanned the kitchen. Still no Jack. Erin needed to leave, but Ziggy was still scratching at the bottom of the sink. She spotted Jack's fridge magnets on the fridge.

Chapter 4
Wheel of Destiny

Erin jumped from magnet to magnet until she reached the kitchen mat. She had replaced a wheel on her skates last week and the old wheel was still on the mat!

Erin squeezed herself into the wheel. She kicked her legs against the kitchen table with a thud and she was off, racing along the hall to her bedroom!

Erin reached up and grabbed the end of a blanket to get to the top of the bed. "If I can just make it to the top of the bed, maybe I'll be able to spot Jack..."

RESCUE   Book 3

Rainbow Fish

Reading Practice

o-e	ow	o
hole	row	no
rope	know	go
home	show	most
close	flow	post
slope	snow	hero
stone	narrow	zero
lonely	elbow	joking
probe	below	broken

oa

boat	moan	
goal	groan	
float	coast	

oe

foe

toes

Contents

Vocabulary:

tumble – to roll end over end when falling

shoal – a large number of fish swimming together

nudge – to push slightly or gently

probe – to search carefully

jagged – with sharp, pointed edges

inch – to move by very small amounts

Erin sat on the pillow to think. She gazed at the glowing fish tank next to the bed. "Oh no, Jack!" she groaned.

Erin had seen a flash of red cloth floating in the fish tank. Was it Jack's sock? She jumped onto the shelf and gazed into the tank.

Had Jack tumbled into the tank? For a second, Erin froze in panic. "Focus," she told herself. "I must find a way to get in that tank!"

Erin was sitting in the middle of a row of dolls. Along the row, a doll was in swimming gear. It just fitted Erin!

Chapter 2
In the tank

"I will hold onto this ice-cream stick to probe the bottom of the tank," said Erin. She held her nose and jumped in.

A shoal of rainbow fish floated so close to Erin that they tickled her. Red and yellow fish followed her and nudged her toes. "Get off!" giggled Erin as the fish swam off.

Erin swam below the bubbles, aiming for the stones at the bottom of the tank. She swam from stone to stone, probing the holes between the rocks in case Jack was trapped there.

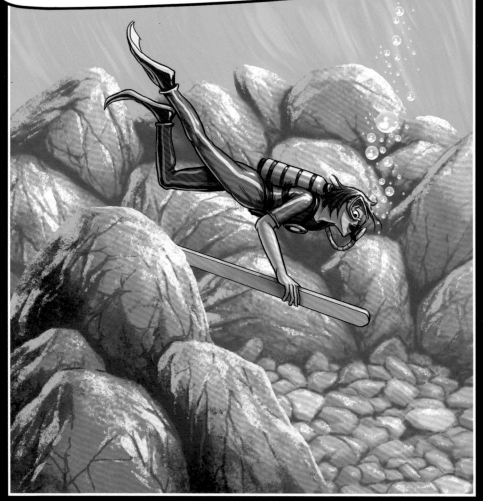

Chapter 3
Is Jack in the Tank?

She stopped at a plastic barrel with jagged holes in it. She poked and probed at the holes with her stick.

Suddenly, a shadow fell over Erin as a massive fish floated over her. "That fish is as big as a whale," groaned Erin.

Erin grabbed a plastic jellyfish and ducked inside it. She kept her legs as still as stone. The fish bumped against her elbow as it swam past, but it did not spot her.

Chapter 4
A Boat!

Erin reached a model boat, shipwrecked on a heap of stones. The red cloth she had seen from the top of the tank was a flag on the boat. It was not Jack's sock. Jack was not in the fish tank!

"I need to get back to the dry land," said Erin with relief. She tugged the boat free and swam up to the top of the tank, dragging it along by its rope.

"I know it is only a model boat. I hope it can float and isn't full of holes," groaned Erin. She let it go at the top of the tank and it bobbed gently in the bubbles.

Chapter 5
Row the Boat Home

Erin jumped into the little boat and rowed it slowly across the tank with the stick. Fish swam along below her.

She grabbed the end of the hose that was hanging over the tank. Slowly, she inched her way up, each moment bringing her closer to home.

At last she was safely back on land. "I'm so glad Jack was not in that fish tank," she told the row of dolls, "but I must keep looking."

RESCUE   Book 4

On with the Search

Reading Practice

er	ur	ir
her	hurt	sir
serve	curl	girl
nerve	turn	bird
stern	burn	first
over	church	stir
finger	disturb	twirl
sister		whirl

or	ear
word	earn
world	search
worth	pearl
work	heard
worm	early

Contents

Vocabulary:

racked her brains – tried very hard to think

nursery – a baby's bedroom

totter – to walk in a shaky, unsteady way

clamber – to climb using both hands and feet

nuzzle – to lie very close to someone or something

clatter – a loud, rattling noise

lurch – sudden staggering or leaning movement

sturdy – strong

gurgle – low bubbling noise made by water flowing

Chapter 1
The Search

Erin had searched all over. She racked her brains. "Please don't let him be hurt," she whispered, as she ran back along the hall and into his nursery.

Erin sat on Jack's bed. She needed to think like him, so she gazed at his things. Jack's rabbit, Jojo, was in his cage next to her.

Jojo was a great pet. He was easy to feed and happy to be held and cuddled. He had never bitten Erin or Jack. Maybe Jack had tottered into Jojo's hutch?

Erin crept over to the hutch and the sleeping rabbit. As she clambered across the metal rungs, she slipped and fell, landing on top of Jojo!

Chapter 2
Jojo Wakes Up!

Jojo stirred and woke up when he felt a girl as big as a carrot land on him! Erin patted his soft fur with her trembling fingers. Jojo sniffed and nuzzled against her.

Erin searched the cage. No Jack. She sat in the soft hay to think. Jojo lay next to her, munching a chunk of red pepper. She gazed at his strong back legs and big feet. "You can help me," she whispered.

She clambered onto Jojo's back and kicked at the pin holding the hutch shut. It was a risky plan, but it was worth the risk if it led her to Jack.

Chapter 3
Searching the Attic

The silver pin dropped with a clatter and Jojo raced along the hall. The eager rabbit began to clamber up the steep steps that led to the attic.

Erin clung on to Jojo's thick fur as he lurched up the steps. A sturdy rabbit and a girl as big as a doll made a great team! "Rabbits make the best roller coasters!" giggled Erin.

As Jojo reached the top of the steps, Erin heard a sob and turned. Jack! Her search was over. She jumped off Jojo's back and ran as fast as the wind.

Erin heard another whimper. It came from the sink in the shower room. Jack must be in the sink! "Jack!" yelled Erin as she clambered up to the sink.

"Jack! I am sending Burt, the rubber duck, to help you! Stand back!" she yelled, as she kicked the plug into the sink. Then she kicked the duck in too.

The plug landed in the plug hole and Burt, the duck, fell on top. "Get on Burt's back," yelled Erin as she set to work turning the water on. At last she did it.

Water splashed into the sink. It gurgled and swirled, filling the sink to the top. "Hold on to Burt!" yelled Erin. Jack held on firmly to the duck.

Jack clung on to the slippery duck as it twirled in circles. He rose closer and closer to the surface. Erin grabbed him when he reached the top and hugged him. "My baby surfer," she grinned.

It had been a big day for Jack. First, he had shrunk himself. Then he had ridden a spider all the way from Mom's desk to the slippery sink. Erin had not seen the spider. She was just glad Jack was safe.

RESCUE   Book 5

A Long Way Down

Reading Practice

ow	ou
cow	out
owl	our
now	mouth
howl	pouch
brown	bound
power	ground
scowl	about

oi	oy
oil	boy
boil	toy
coin	destroy
voice	annoy
spoil	enjoy

Contents

Vocabulary:

bounded – leapt

antidote – a remedy or cure for an unwanted effect

descent – going downwards

mound – a pile or heap

pounce – to leap on

spun – to twist around

Chapter 1
A Long Way Down

Jack sat down with a bump. His mouth turned down and his bottom lip began to quiver. "Stay strong, baby boy," whispered Erin as she hugged him.

Erin grabbed a toothbrush and jumped onto it. She galloped around Jack, making sounds like a donkey. Jack chuckled.

2

Jack giggled as Erin bounded around him. Erin held out the lid from a bottle of bubble bath. "You can feed the donkey now," she told him.

Erin frowned. How was she going to keep Jack safe? Then she grinned. They just needed to get back down to the antidote. "I can be the donkey!"

The Descent

Jack was giggling when Erin lifted him onto her back. "I am the donkey now!" she told him in a silly voice.

A towel was hanging under the sink. Erin climbed down it with Jack clinging to her back, his little round face pressed against her.

Erin clambered down the attic steps with Jack on her back. It was a bumpy trip, but at last they reached solid ground again. Jack was sniffing. "We can eat now," Erin whispered.

Chapter 3
The Antidote

Erin found the picnic she had made. Jack ate a mound of apple chunks as Erin tugged the lid off the bottle of antidote.

Erin was just about to feed Jack the oily green liquid when she was distracted by an odd growling sound. She turned round just as Ziggy was about to pounce!

Erin crumpled a chunk of foil into a ball and hurled it at Ziggy. "Quick, Jack, we must run NOW!" she shouted. They got away, but the liquid spilled on the ground!

They ran and hid in the closet. Erin kicked the empty bottle and scowled. Without the antidote, they had nothing to reverse the shrinking. Suddenly, she remembered something Mom had told her.

"I think this electric pod will reverse the shrinking," Mom had told her. The pod was still on Mom's desk. Twisted cables snaked around it.

How was she going to get Jack to sit in the pod? She rolled a big round candy into it and sat down and licked it. Jack grinned and began to lick it too.

Erin needed to connect the pod to some energy. She grabbed a cable and pushed it into the socket behind them. She took hold of Jack and held him close as they spun around.

Erin was dizzy and boiling hot. Had she been sleeping? She gazed around her. Jack was asleep in her lap, but they were not in the pod. Clouds surrounded them. Her chest began to pound.

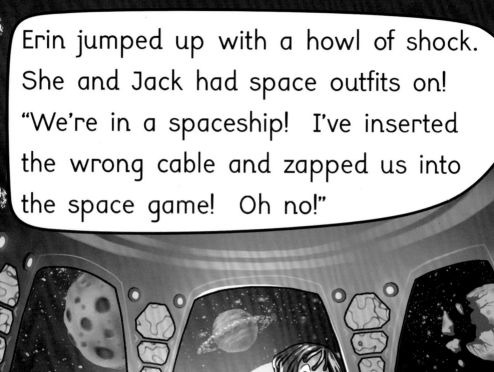

Erin jumped up with a howl of shock. She and Jack had space outfits on! "We're in a spaceship! I've inserted the wrong cable and zapped us into the space game! Oh no!"

RESCUE   Book 6
A Gruesome Monster

Reading Practice

oo	ou	ew
too	you	chew
soon	soup	grew
cool	youth	drew
swoop	group	flew
scoop		threw
foolish		

u	ue	u–e
truth	clue	rude
July	blue	rule
super	true	brute
	gruesome	include
		conclude

Contents

Vocabulary:

ponder — to think carefully about something

soothing — calming, comforting

chute — a tilted tube

jolt — to knock sharply

doomed — going to die

Chapter 1
Zapped!

Erin gazed at her blue and red space outfit. It was all still true. The electric pod had not helped them grow. It had zapped them into the space game that she and Danny had been playing!

Jack was snoozing next to her. They were trapped in a spaceship and Erin did not know what to do. "I must search this spaceship for clues," she whispered.

A row of buttons glowed on a big screen next to a window. "Maybe I need to choose one," she pondered. Erin crossed her fingers and pressed a flashing blue button.

The button was round and smooth. At first it felt cool and soothing under her hand. Then it turned red and began to throb.

Chapter 2
Space Terror!

A jet of freezing cold air blew down a chute. Suddenly, the spaceship jolted. The movement threw them across the room. "Hold on, Jack!" yelled Erin.

A gruesome space monster loomed over the spaceship. His cruel voice boomed across the galaxy. "You fools have set me free! I am free to destroy you two and every living thing on this planet."

The space monster's cruel face filled the screen. Erin gazed in terror as his eyes and mouth began to glow red. He began to chew on the spaceship.

Chapter 3
Escape

They had to escape from the spaceship or they were doomed. Erin scanned the buttons on the screen. "Down!" said Jack, and his wriggling leg kicked a button.

A tube of rings shot down from the roof of the ship. It sucked Jack and Erin into it. Whoosh! In a second, it had pulled them up and out through the roof of the ship!

The tube took them into the moonlit galaxy! Erin screamed. This must be the end – something very odd was happening. "We are floating in space!" she yelled. "Jack! We have super powers!"

The monster hadn't seen Erin and Jack zoom out of the spaceship. He was still chewing at the ship with his gruesome teeth. It was too big for him to chew and his mouth got stuck around it.

Erin's plans did not include a rude space monster with toothache! "Let's fly away, baby Jack," she shouted. They flew smoothly along and aimed for a planet made completely of food!

They landed with a bump under a spotted toadstool. Erin scooped up a handful of soft noodles to feed Jack. "If we stay much longer, we can make noodle soup," she joked.

13

Chapter 4
A Way Out

Erin and Jack sheltered under a ring of mushrooms. A galaxy full of planets was fun to zoom around, but it was not home. They needed to find a way out of this mad game.

She and Danny had played this game all summer. She knew it well. The food planet was the first level. The second level was the planet of jewels. They had to get through both to win the game.

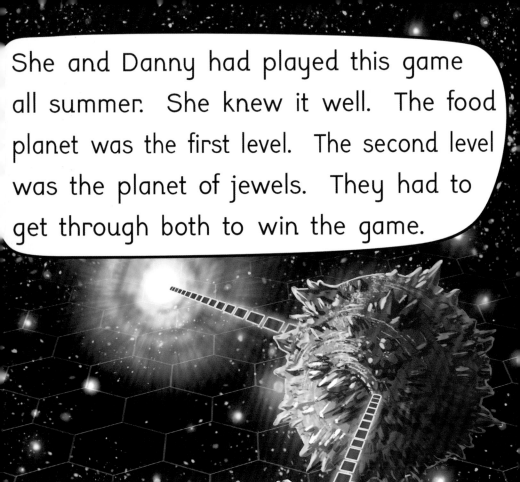

Erin checked the energy cell on her heel. It flashed. She only had three cells left to use. They needed to get to the end of the game soon.

16

RESCUE   Book 7

Time is Running Out!

Reading Practice

igh	i	i-e
light	find	time
might	wild	life
tight	climb	pipe
right	spider	hide
flight	giant	while
fright	behind	smile
		stripe

ie	y
die	my
tie	by
cried	try
tried	fly
	crying

Contents

Vocabulary:

glide   – to move smoothly and easily along

twirled   – turned round and round quickly

swirling – twisting, spinning

duck   – to bend or move out of the way of

                 something

cunning – sly and clever

beam   – to grin

glint   – to shine brightly

Chapter 1
The Golden Slice

Time was running out. Erin had just three life cells left and they were still trapped in the first level of Space Time. She hugged Jack tight.

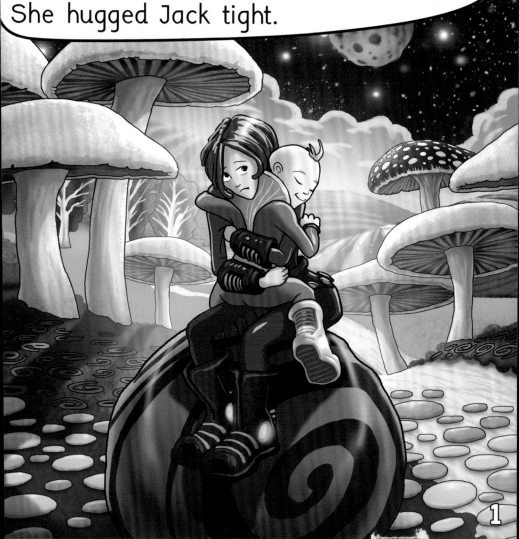

"We need to find a golden slice of cake. Then we can cross the divide between the levels and enter the final level of the game," she told him. Suddenly, she spotted a giant cake!

2

The cake was the size of a mountain! They glided closer to it. Cakes of all shapes and sizes twirled around it like the tide. Every type of cake, except the golden slice.

"I need to find that golden slice!" Erin bounced high up in the sky. Below them stretched a swirling line of cakes and at the end of it was the golden slice!

4

Chapter 2
Catch It If You Can!

If Erin tried to grab the cake slice, it might run away. The best plan was to hide and try to catch it as it floated by. They hid behind a cupcake that was the size of a house.

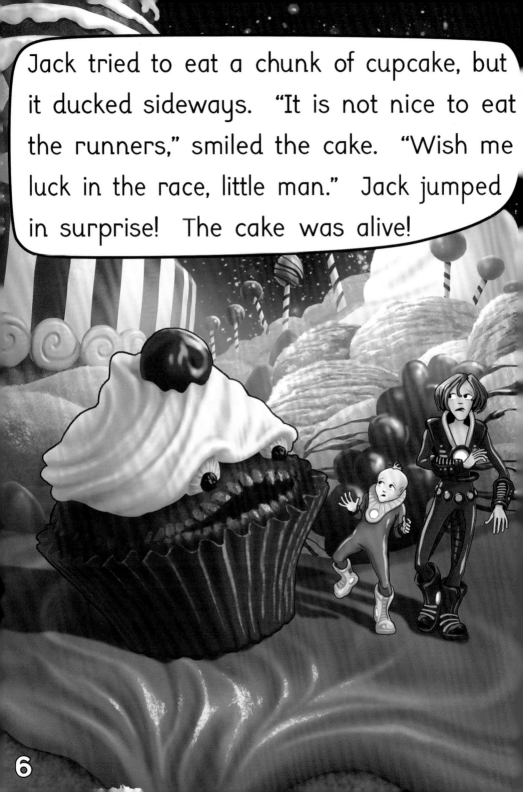

Jack tried to eat a chunk of cupcake, but it ducked sideways. "It is not nice to eat the runners," smiled the cake. "Wish me luck in the race, little man." Jack jumped in surprise! The cake was alive!

Race day! Erin had played this level at home. On race day, the golden slice of cake was the top prize in the race! "I have to win the race and win the slice!" she cried.

Chapter 3
Cunning Disguise!

They needed to disguise themselves to join the race. Jack had found a heap of candies shaped like flowers. Erin grabbed a sheet of thick white icing from the ground and wrapped it tightly around them.

The cakes lined up. It was a tight fit and Erin had to fight for a space. She and Jack sped off. Suddenly, the sheet of icing was tugged off them by a gust of wind!

A striped cake stopped to help. "We need to escape from this level," sobbed Erin. "If we die in the game, then we will never get home alive!"

"I might be tiny, but I can get you to the finish line," beamed Stripe, the cake. "Hold tight!" he grinned, and set off at the speed of light. Soon Erin and Jack were flying along!

11

An apple pie crashed into Stripe's side. Cake crumbs lay in the dust. "My time is up!" sighed Stripe. "A cake my size can't survive a crash like that!"

Suddenly, a shadow fell over the race and a giant face filled the sky. Erin was terrified, but Jack giggled with delight and gurgled, "Dan Dan". Danny was outside the screen, gazing in!

13

Chapter 4
Danny's Game

Danny began to play the game as if his life depended on it. He healed the broken cake and sent it flying back along the track. Erin and Jack bobbed along in the sky behind it like kites.

Stripe won the race! Danny had saved them just in time! "Take the prize, Erin. Thanks to Danny, I am still alive!" grinned the happy cake.

Erin hugged Jack as they crossed over the line to the final level. The planet of jewels glinted brightly. It was going to be alright. This time, they had Danny on their side.

RESCUE   Book 8

An Awful Planet

Reading Practice

a	**aw**	**au**
all	saw	maul
call	claw	haunt
small	straw	August
almost	draw	assault
	awful	

awe	**al**	**ough**
awe	walk	fought
awesome	talk	thought

Contents

Vocabulary:

awe — fear and wonder

scorching — very hot

swarm — large numbers of animals or creatures moving together

maul — to bite or claw at like a wild animal

toxic — poisonous

torment — to cause suffering

scale — to climb

transform — to change into something quite different

portal — an entry point

orbit — to move around something in a circular path

Chapter 1
Planet of Jewels

Erin gazed at the planet of jewels in awe. Jack was keen to explore the gleaming jewels swimming before them. He scrambled down from Erin's hip and began to crawl forward.

The planet was scorching hot! Erin grabbed Jack and blew on his warm hands before they got sore. A swarm of small jewels formed around them, snapping their jaws!

2

"Danny!" called Erin in panic. "The jewels are alive! I need a safe track!"
"Grab that flashlight on the ground," yelled Danny. "It will draw you a safe track across this awful planet!"

They ran along the track. More jewels tried to maul them with claws like wild animal paws. "I don't want a war!" yelled Erin. "I just want to get us off this toxic planet!"

4

Chapter 2
The Golden Astronaut

As they turned a corner, a tall, spiky jewel jumped onto the track and Erin felt herself falling. "Curl up like a ball, Jack!" she yelled as they fell.

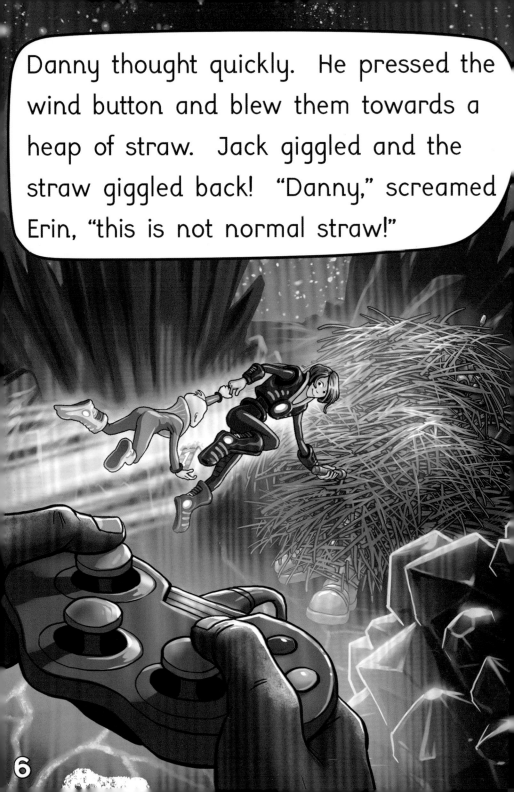

Danny thought quickly. He pressed the wind button and blew them towards a heap of straw. Jack giggled and the straw giggled back! "Danny," screamed Erin, "this is not normal straw!"

6

The heap of straw began to walk across space! It was alive! Erin looked more closely and saw the straw was a disguise being worn by a golden astronaut!

7

Chapter 3
A Golden Ring

"The astronaut is like a lord in this game," called Danny. "We need to find him a golden ring. If we bring him a golden ring and the golden cake, he will have food and cash and you'll win the game."

Danny saw the ring glinting on the top of a tall tree! Jewels swarmed around Erin, tormenting her as she scaled the tree. She fought them off with beams of hot light from the flashlight.

9

Erin tore the golden ring from the top of the tree and clawed her way back down to Jack. The golden cake slice was in her pocket and she handed them both to the golden astronaut.

10

The astronaut held the ring and cake up before him. They transformed into a glowing portal. Erin did not stop to talk to Danny. She and Jack launched themselves into the portal.

Splinters of blazing light shot from the screen like thorns. Danny was hiding his face from them when Erin suddenly crashed into his cheek! She and Jack had been transported!

Transported

Danny rubbed his jaw. "Can you warn me when you are in orbit next time?" he joked. "I'll run into the hall and hide!" Erin hugged him, but she felt sad that they were still so small.

Jack was yawning. "We need to get to the lab and find Mom, before nightfall," said Erin softly.

Danny paused, deep in thought. "We can go on my skateboard!"

Jack crawled into Danny's pocket and was soon snoring. Danny grabbed his skateboard from the porch. "Let me sit in your hat," begged Erin. "I can see more and we can talk."

"How do we get to the lab?" asked Danny. "I'll show you the way. Shame I forgot that magic flashlight," yelled Erin. They set off for the lab, a boy on a skateboard, a girl tucked into his hat, and a tiny boy snoring in his pocket.

RESCUE   Book 10

Dark Times

Reading Practice

car	dark
art	sharp
card	hard
farm	shards
star	afar
shark	arches
alarm	guard
mark	large
yard	barbed
	darted

Contents

Vocabulary:

snarling – growling threateningly

rustling – making slight, soft sounds when things rub together

blade – the broad part of a leaf

harsh – unpleasant

rasping – an unpleasant sound made by things rubbing roughly together

shards – fragments or small pieces of something

scanned – looked at or examined

darted – moved swiftly

Chapter 1
The Garden

Erin lowered herself out of Polly's window and into the garden. Flowers stretched far into the distance. She started to search for a way across.

The evening sun cast a shadow over the garden and Erin shivered at the sound of a snarling dog. "It will be dark soon," she thought. "I'd rather not be stuck in this jungle then."

A rustling noise distracted her. Was it a cat? Erin's heart thumped in her chest. But it was just an army of ants marching along a blade of grass.

Crumbs of almond cake wobbled on the ants' backs. Erin was starving, so she grabbed a chunk of cake as the ants marched past.

Chapter 2
The Phone

Suddenly, a harsh, rasping noise filled the garden. Erin ran for shelter. It was a lawn mower! She ran deeper into the flower bed.

Shards of bark rained down on the grass as an old man walked past with the mower. He had hit a log in the grass. When he stopped to unblock the mower, Erin spotted a phone in his jacket.

This was her chance! Erin ran across the grass as fast as the wind. She jumped up onto the phone and pressed Mom's number on the keys.

Outside the lab, Mom scanned the evening sky. The light was fading fast and they needed to find Erin before any harm came to her. She tried to keep calm and think of a plan.

Suddenly something started to ring in her pocket. Her heart skipped a beat when she heard Erin's tiny voice on her phone! "Where are you?" she asked with a gasp.

The garden full of flowers! Mom had walked past it on her way to work. It was halfway between the lab and home. She grabbed Danny's arm. "Go by skateboard, Dan. It will be much faster."

Danny flew like the wind. He darted across the park and skidded to a stop outside the old man's garden. Erin was waiting for him on the fence.

Danny laughed when he saw Erin's wings and the flower in her hair! "I like it," he grinned. "It's a pity you can't keep it as a party outfit!"

Saved!

It was starting to get dark by the time they were back at the lab. Jack laughed out loud at the sight of Erin as a fairy! Erin did a little dance on the palm of Danny's hand.

Mom held Erin gently in the palm of her hand to give her the antidote. "You are so brave, darling. You had a hard choice to make when Jack got shrunk and you chose to save him."

In a flash, Erin was full size again! Mom locked the shrink ray away in a safe in the lab. "I hope this is the last we ever see of it," she told Erin.

Later that night, Erin and Danny lay on the grass in the garden. Stars danced in the dark sky. "I learned some great moves inside that space game," murmured Erin. "Maybe next time we play it, I'll play from inside again!"